Can I Have My Ball Back?

'Can I Have My Ball Back?'
An original concept by Alice Hemming
© Alice Hemming

Illustrated by Ed Myer

Published by MAVERICK ARTS PUBLISHING LTD

Studio 3A, City Business Centre, 6 Brighton Road,

Horsham, West Sussex, RH13 5BB

© Maverick Arts Publishing Limited May 2017

+44 (0)1403 256941

A CIP catalogue record for this book is available at the British Library.

ISBN 978-1-84886-252-4

www.maverickbooks.co.uk

Yellow

This book is rated as: Yellow Band (Guided Reading)
This story is decodable at Letters and Sounds Phase 3.

Can I Have My Ball Back?

by **Alice Hemming**
illustrated by **Ed Myer**

Mr Ricket has a new shed.

It is near the park.

A ball hits the shed.

Mr Ricket's
Shed

He sends it back.

Balls hit the shed roof. 'Boing! boing!'

He kicks them back.

Lots of things zoom into the garden.

Mr Ricket's
Shed

Mr Ricket gets all the things.

He sends them back.

Mr Ricket is fed up.

Mr Ricket has a good plan.

It is a new invention.

Amazing Ball Chucker

Amazing Ball Chuc

Quiz

1. Where is Mr Ricket's new shed?
a) Near a lake
b) In a forest
c) By the park

2. What does Mr Ricket keep in his shed?
a) His inventions
b) His car
c) His gardening tools

3. What happens when lots of things hit the shed?
a) The shed is broken
b) The inventions go wrong
c) Mr Ricket goes into his house

4. What does Mr Ricket invent?

a) A ball throwing machine

b) A shed with wheels

c) A cleaning robot

5. What noise do the balls make when they hit the roof?

a) Bang

b) Boing

c) Crash

Turn over for answers

- Pink
- Red (End of Yr R)
- Yellow
- Blue
- Green
- Orange
- Turquoise (End of Yr 1)
- Purple
- Gold
- White (End of Yr 2)
- Lime

Book Bands for Guided Reading

The Institute of Education book banding system is made up of twelve colours, which reflect the level of reading difficulty. The bands are assigned by taking into account the content, the language style, the layout and phonics.

Children learn at different speeds but the colour chart shows the levels of progression with the national expectation shown in brackets. To learn more visit the IoE website: www.ioe.ac.uk.

All of these books have been book banded for guided reading to the industry standard and edited by a leading educational consultant.

For more titles visit: www.maverickbooks.co.uk/early-readers

Quiz Answers: 1c, 2a, 3b, 4a, 5b